To:

From:

Get Well Soon!

words by Erin Guendelsberger
pictures by Joe Mathieu

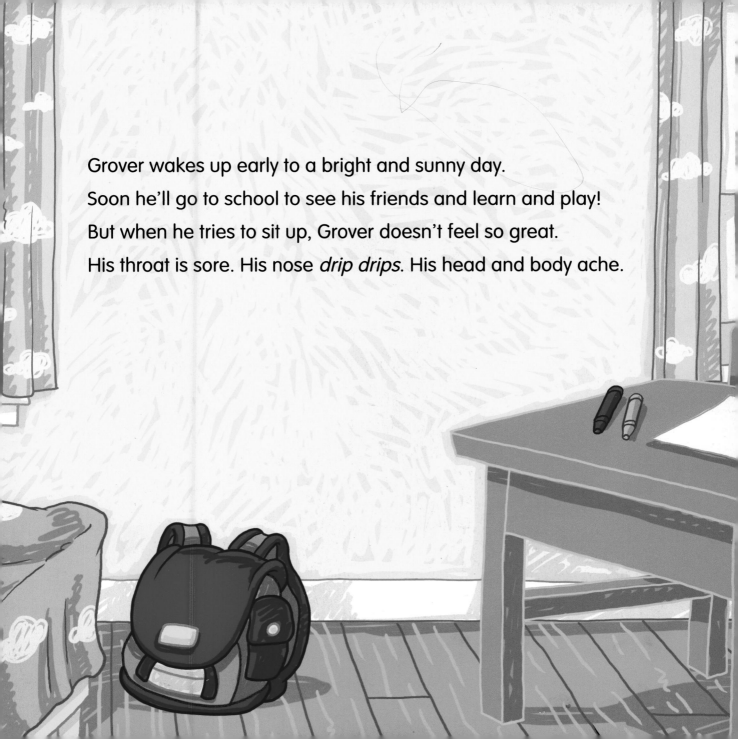

Grover wakes up early to a bright and sunny day.

Soon he'll go to school to see his friends and learn and play!

But when he tries to sit up, Grover doesn't feel so great.

His throat is sore. His nose *drip drips*. His head and body ache.

Grover calls his mommy, and she comes to check what's wrong.

She puts her hand against his head and hums his favorite song.

She uses a thermometer to see what it will say.

Grover has a fever, and he must stay home today.

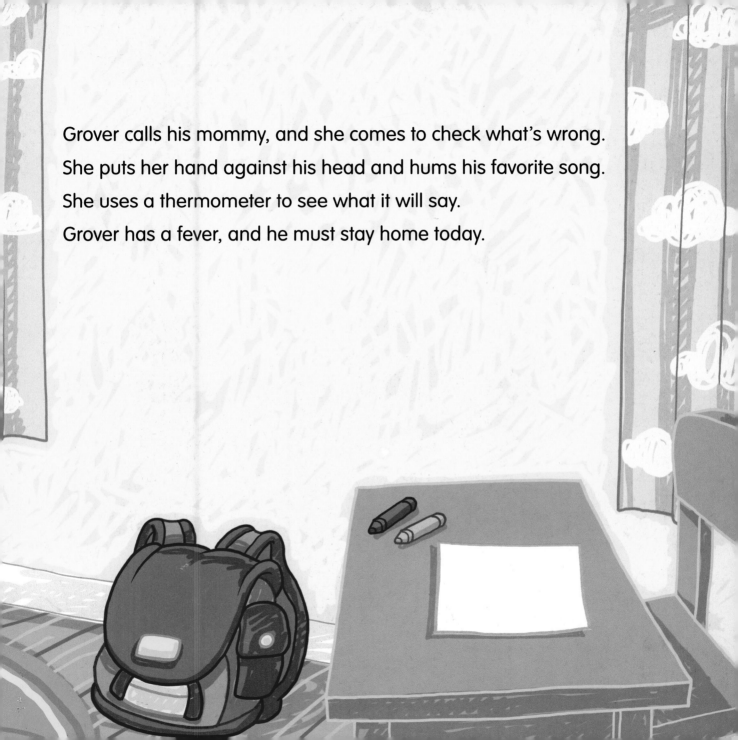

Grover doesn't want to stay!
He wants to go to school.

He's seeing Elmo afterward and visiting the pool.

It's also Grover's turn today to bring in show-and-tell. "I want to take my cape in. Superheroes must stay well!"

But Mommy says that even big strong heroes can get sick.
With lots of rest and water, he'll feel better extra quick.
She says that if he goes to school and plays with Elmo too,
Grover could get others sick, which no one wants to do.

Grover must take medicine, and it tastes really yuck!

Then Mommy lays him down and does his favorite cover tuck.

But the blanket is too heavy! It's not right. Too big! Too tight!

When Mommy tries another, it's too small! Too loose! Too light!

Grover blows his nose—*honk, honk!*—and gives two little sighs.
He snuggles down to rest and then he starts to close his eyes.

His pillow is too hard and thin!
He just can't fall asleep.

And when he tries a new one,
it's too soft and thick and deep.

Grover twists and turns but can't get comfortable enough.

His brand-new blue pajamas are too scratchy, stiff, and rough.

He changes to his green pj's, but still feels rather grumpy.

"These old ones are not right," he says. "Too fuzzy and too lumpy!"

Right outside the window,
birds are making quite a sound.
The noisy cheeps and tweets are making
Grover's headache pound.

Mommy shuts the window tight to keep the noises out.
Now the room is quiet—much *too* quiet—Grover pouts.

Mommy mixes chicken noodle soup up in a pot.

When Grover takes a taste, he cries out, "Ouch! The soup's too hot!"

He waits a while before he tries to take another bite.
Now the soup's too cold! Grover just can't get it right.

Grover tells his mommy he feels icky, yucky, sad.

With nothing going right, he can't feel anything but bad.

Grover gives a big *ACHOOO!* and slumps down in his bed.

Being sick is just no fun! He hangs his monster head.

Mommy says that nothing seems quite right when you feel wrong.

When you are sick, your body needs to rest to come back strong.

Hour by hour and day by day, the body works to heal.

And then before you know it, you'll be shocked how great you feel.

Mommy brings a small surprise to brighten up the room.

It's a card from Elmo saying, "Grover, get well soon!"

Elmo knew that Grover wasn't feeling well that day.

He wants his friend to rest! There will be other times to play.

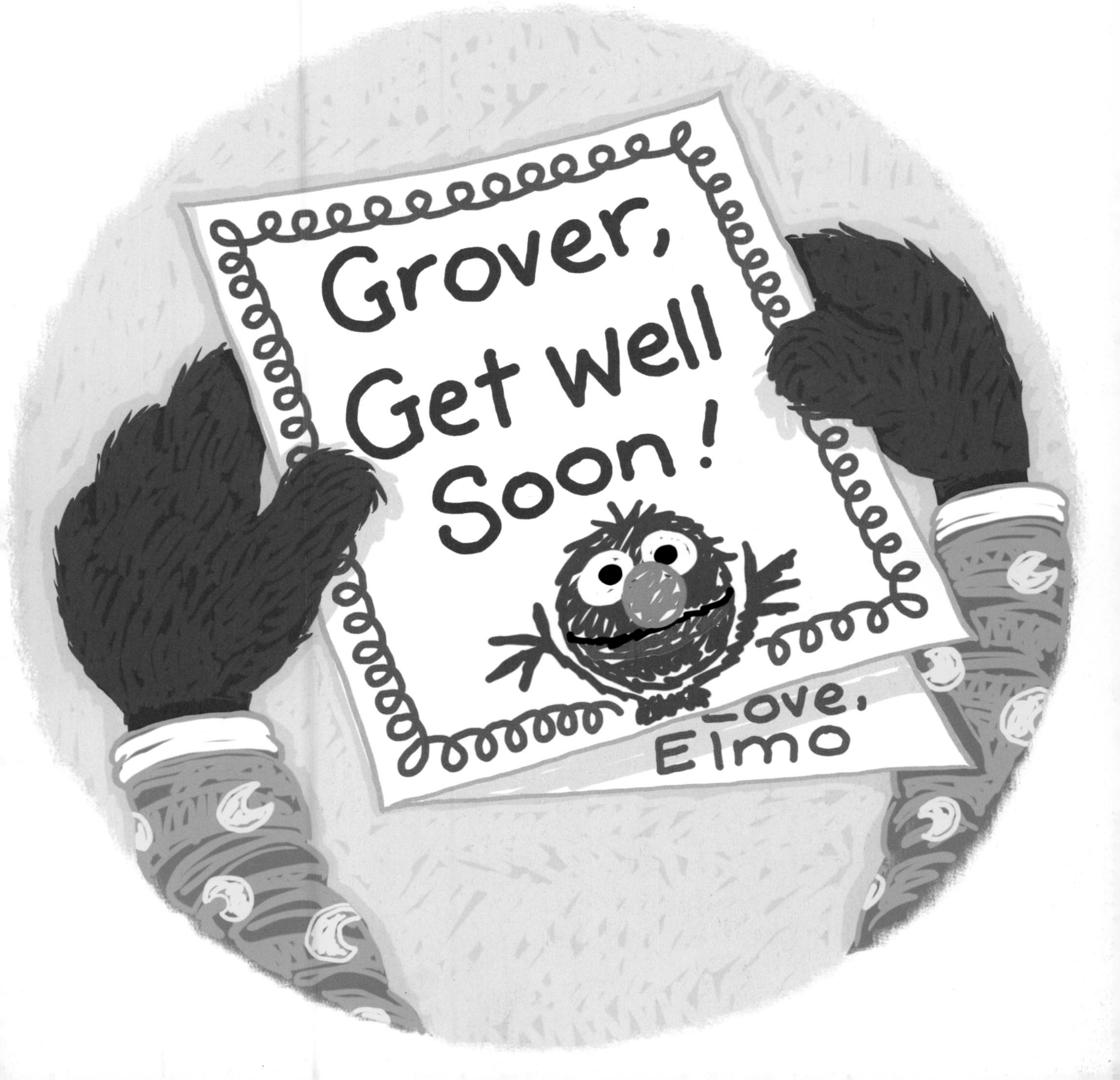
Grover,
Get Well
Soon!
Love,
Elmo

Grover loves his special card! He sets it by his light.

With Mommy and his card nearby, things start to feel "just right."

He puts on *both* his blankets, and he stretches big and tall.

They're not too tight or loose, and they're not too big or small.

He fluffs his pillows—*puff, puff, puff!*—until they're nice and plump.

He smooths his jammies—*tug, tug, tug!* There are no lumps or bumps.

Mommy plays some music,
not too loud or soft—just fine.

She heats up Grover's soup.
It's not too hot or cold this time.

Grover finally falls asleep and spends the day in bed.

He wakes up feeling better in his throat and nose and head.

For a few more days, he takes it easy, getting lots of rest.

With sleep and Mommy hugs,
at last he starts to feel his best.

Grover,
Get Well
Soon

Rx

It's hard when you've been feeling sick and nothing seems quite right.
But then you wake one morning, and the world looks new and bright.
Grover feels all better now—in fact, he's feeling great!
"Now I can play with Elmo, and it sure was worth the wait!"

Cover and internal design © 2020 by Sourcebooks
Text by Erin Guendelsberger
Illustrations by Joe Mathieu

Sourcebooks and the colophon are registered trademarks of Sourcebooks.

Published by Sourcebooks Wonderland, an imprint of Sourcebooks Kids
P.O. Box 4410, Naperville, Illinois 60567-4410
(630) 961-3900
sourcebookskids.com

Source of Production: Wing King Tong Paper Products Co. Ltd., Shenzhen, Guangdong Province, China
Date of Production: March 2020
Run Number: 5017861

Printed and bound in China.
WKT 10 9 8 7 6 5 4 3 2 1